D0326854

THE
JAMES
MIRACLE

* * *

Other Books by Jason F. Wright
Published by Shadow Mountain

Christmas Jars
Christmas Jars Reunion
Penny's Christmas Jar Miracle
Recovering Charles
The 13th Day of Christmas
The Wedding Letters
The Wednesday Letters

THE
JAMES
MIRACLE

JASON F. WRIGHT

SHADOW
MOUNTAIN

Original Text © 2004 Jason F. Wright
Revised Text © 2014 Jason F. Wright

All rights reserved. No part of this book may be reproduced in any form or by any means without permission in writing from the publisher, Shadow Mountain®, at permissions@shadowmountain.com or P. O. Box 30178, Salt Lake City, Utah 84130. The views expressed herein are the responsibility of the author and do not necessarily represent the position of Shadow Mountain.

All characters in this book are fictitious, and any resemblance to actual persons, living or dead, is purely coincidental.

Visit us at ShadowMountain.com

Library of Congress Cataloging-in-Publication Data

Wright, Jason F., author.

  The James miracle / Jason F. Wright.

    pages cm

  Summary: Sam and Holly Foster never expected the hardship that caused their perfect world to shatter. It will take the miracle of their young son James's toy boat and a mysterious man to remind them that heaven is not far and that love is never lost.—Provided by publisher

  ISBN 978-1-60907-931-4 (hardbound : alk. paper)

1. Unemployment—Fiction. 2. Children—Death—Fiction. 3. Miracles—Fiction. I. Title.

  PS3623.R539J36 2014

  813'.6—dc23   2014017572

Printed in the United States of America
Publishers Printing, Salt Lake City, UT

10   9   8   7   6   5   4   3   2   1

R0442086012

For my dear wife, Kodi,
who will always be my miracle

Dear Reader,

On December 24, 2003, I visited a copy shop and had them print and bind one copy of a manuscript I'd secretly been writing before work, during lunch, and when my small family slept in our home in Fairfax, Virginia.

It was *The James Miracle*.

Later that night, I wrapped the flimsy, comb-bound book with its card stock cover and slid it under our Christmas tree. I'd never been so excited to give a gift!

The next morning, after our two little girls had opened their presents, I handed the package to my wife and nervously watched her open it. Her eyes went wide at the dedication and title page. "You wrote this?" she asked, flipping through the pages. *"All of it?"*

I laughed and assured her it was an original work. Then I explained that the book wasn't really the gift—it was the message. There were things I needed to say, and this novella had become my outlet for saying them. I watched her read it in one sitting that afternoon, and I suspect many of you will read it in one sitting, too. (Though I promise I won't be watching!)

In 2004, the novella was released in a very limited print run. And, against all odds, a writing career was born.

Much has changed in the decade since, and many more

books have landed on shelves and e-readers, but *The James Miracle* will always hold a special place in my heart and in hers.

Thank you for giving it another life in this special ten-year anniversary edition. Mostly, thank you for believing in miracles.

Jason

PS: This book wouldn't have seen sunlight without a few special people. First and foremost, my brother Jeff provided endless encouragement and feedback as I fumbled along. Thanks also to Kodi, Sterling, Terilynne, and my mother, Sandi Lou, for reading and critiquing this novel—and everything I've written since. I couldn't ask for a better, more brutally honest focus group. I love you all.

Thanks, also, to Janeal Rogers, Ryan and Randy Bott, Sheri Dew, Chris Schoebinger, Laurel Christensen Day, Heidi Taylor, and Lisa Mangum for publishing me and inviting me to be a better writer and, more importantly, a better person.

MIRACLES

A very wise philosopher once said over hot caramel sundaes after middle school graduation: "Life's miracles happen when you least expect them." He said it wasn't the well-planned, made-for-television moments that change and define us. Instead, our destiny is determined by how we choose to weave into our lives the random, unexpected happenings on seemingly normal Thursday afternoons. "Be prepared for chance, change, and miracles," he offered with a wise wink. He preached that miracles would come in a thousand and one different packages. "And some will feel better on your soul than others," he finished with a wrinkled smile, tapping the end of my nose with his dripping oversized dessertspoon.

Sadly, that wise man died when I was too young to fully appreciate his wisdom. It's a shame; my father was a genius.

It's been years since he left behind an arrogant, selfish son for a pain-free career well beyond the clouds. My mother told us that cancer had not beaten him. He had beaten it.

Forever.

"Chins up, gang," she consoled in the back of a slick black limousine. "He could have let it run our family for thirty years, but he simply would not let that happen. That brave man kicked it right out of our lives. And now he's closer than ever. He's in our hearts." Then she offered a prayer, nodded to the driver, and we watched through the tinted rear window as the caravan of headlights cut through traffic.

Since that soggy afternoon, I've learned to believe that he now enjoys an endless supply of perfect summer days when golf scores are low and mid-afternoon watermelon tastes like it was grown in heaven. And every night his favorite pillow smells just like Mom.

But most importantly, I have come to fully appreciate how right Dad was about chance, change, and miracles.

At any given second, somewhere in this grand old world of His, someone kneels beside a bed, or a couch, or inside a mildewed cardboard box underneath some remote highway overpass, and asks, "God, do miracles exist?"

They do.

And not just on Thursday afternoons.

FAMILIES

I am Sam Foster. You can call me Average.

It is a truth I cannot escape; I have been mediocre at nearly everything I've ever attempted. I have been average at athletics, academics, and even in matters of spirituality. Regardless of what my parents said, I knew the teachers and advisers were right. I was just good enough, just smart enough, and just fast enough to coast along unburdened by weighty expectations. It seems I am forever that young, pimple-faced student by which all others were measured and made exceptional by comparison.

In nearly every way imaginable I have been—and fear I always will be—vanilla.

"The Foster Four," as Mom and Dad called the kids, were raised just outside the nation's capital in northern Virginia. On their own, my parents might have been judged as unspectacular, but as a pair they worked miracles. Together we lived in a humble home the Realtor had insisted was built for a mom, a dad, and two kids—max. But they decided to have four and call the challenge a "test of our mettle."

It was a test all right; my brothers and I tested their homeowner's policy many times over the years. The sound of breaking glass was as common as the dinner bell.

While the others joined the marching band, played on the basketball team, or dominated the school science fair, I spent my extracurricular hours picking fights with bigger kids behind the green center-field fence of the baseball field, just so I could hone my ability to talk my way out of them. I became famous for fights that ended with handshakes and deals, not punches. Somehow I escaped delivering or receiving a single black eye or swollen lip during those adolescent years.

"The key, Sam," my father counseled, "is finding something you're good at and convincing someone to pay you to do it." Then his eyes would smile brightly and he'd add, "Sam, you could sell sand at a desert flea market."

I committed to always work harder than those around me; my parents expected tremendous success from the youngest of the Foster Four. And while I seldom took the most conventional route from one point to the next, once there I could always close the deal. People would learn to count on me, they would need me, and I would deliver.

Just weeks after Dad died I sat alone after school in a quiet classroom. On the inside cover of my twelfth-grade economics textbook, I made a goal to persuade everyone I ever met that spending time to know me would be a wise investment. "I, Samuel T. Foster, will create *The Sam Show*," I scribbled in bad cursive. And the entire world would buy tickets.

Then came Holly.

She was the one who proved the exception to every rule I'd ever established. She would see through the sheer curtains of my show from the opening act.

How I would love her for it.

✳ ✳ ✳

Holly Walker was raised by a sweet Southern belle in Charleston, West Virginia. Her father had gone off to Vietnam when she was just a few years old and never returned. The army called him "missing in action," but for years Holly's mother spoke of him returning. Even long after the conflict was over, Holly's mother kept his clothes in the closet and a pair of black slippers by his side of the bed. But Holly had known by the time she was six or seven that he would never return.

Nevertheless, she allowed her mother to lose herself in the fantasy of a heroic return.

While her mother's mind lived in the wet jungles of Asia, Holly became a caretaker for her younger sister. Holly was cooking simple meals and helping with homework by the third grade. By fourteen she was driving around the quiet streets on the outskirts of Charleston, juggling two paper routes and taking her mother to and from a handful of women's support groups.

In the rare moments when not playing guardian, Holly buried herself in schoolwork and read nearly every book in the small city library. "Your father's dream," her mother said during one of their last lucid conversations, "is to return from the war, put down his gun, and become a teacher." Holly made that dream her own, and her dogged determination landed her the top spot in her graduating class of 195 students and a scholarship to Georgetown University in the heart of Washington, D.C.

The Thursday before classes began, she packed everything she owned into two oversized canvas bags and prepared to board a bus for the half-day trip to the nation's capital. "You can do this," she said, holding tightly to her sister, now a high school sophomore. She kissed her mother on the cheek, told her she loved her, promised to return home once a month, then wondered if she had any idea what was about to happen.

"Is your daddy on this bus?" Mother asked softly, staring at the silver Greyhound.

"No, Momma." Holly hugged her again. "Not on this one." Then she climbed aboard and watched from the last seat as her sister and mother walked away arm in arm through a thick cloud of gray-blue exhaust.

Holly cried halfway to Washington. Though she was finally leaving Charleston, the tears said her mother had left long ago.

*   *   *

I was headed to another long day on Capitol Hill as an intern with a Florida congressman. I had no interest in a career in politics or public policy, but the business degree I sought from George Mason University in Fairfax, Virginia, required an internship and "on the hill," as they say, was as good a place as any.

The hours were long and the people just friendly enough to survive the daily grind without losing their minds. Of course, I was convinced some already had. Fortunately it took just a few weeks for me to establish myself as an asset to the office, willing to say or do anything at any time, mostly to mask my inadequacies in an environment full of academic whiz kids.

The subway train carried me beneath the streets of D.C., and through the hum of a hundred conversations, I overheard a uniquely mesmerizing voice. "It was like a song," I gushed that night to my incredulous roommates. "Or like the way a white dove might sound, you know, if it could talk."

They mocked me relentlessly for weeks.

Tracing the voice through the crowded train I found a woman of my exact height. She wore a modest, lime-green shirt with what looked like smiley-faced lemons embroidered on the sleeves. Around her waist she'd tied a darker green rain jacket. Though she was twenty feet away, I could easily judge that her eyes were somewhere between caramel and brown sugar. Scanning the other riders, I noted with great disappointment that I was not the only one who had discovered her. She'd captured the rapt attention of a half dozen other men.

I tuned in just as she explained to an inquisitive tourist and her eager, map-wielding husband that she was off to the Library of Congress on an all-day research mission for the professor she assisted three days a week for extra credit—and a few extra dollars. I memorized every word the woman spoke and felt myself wrapped in a comfortable sense that *change and chance*, as Dad always said, had arrived.

The curious, wide-eyed tourists exited at the Smithsonian Museum stop. As the train pulled away I slipped carefully between a baby stroller and a courier singing and bobbing in reggae rhythm to his portable compact disc player. "Excuse me." I slid the staff identification card hanging from my neck into my crisp shirt pocket. "Do you know where the Library of Congress is?" Everyone in Washington not wearing a fanny pack or carrying a camera knows where to find the Library of Congress. In fact, I knew it better than most; it was across the street from the office building I worked in six and sometimes seven days a week.

"Sure do. I'm headed there myself. I'll lead you all the way to the front door, but you're on your own from there." The corners of her rose-colored lips lifted her entire face. That moment remains perfectly filed in my mind's scrapbook, like a child's first Christmas memory.

We rode up the long escalator together from the subway into a sun-drenched morning. I tried to learn as much about her as possible in the five-minute walk to the large white nondescript building she would spend her day in. "If this is twenty questions," she quipped as we said good-bye, "you're way over the limit!"

I spent that afternoon plotting with a fellow greenie intern how I might find her again without actually enrolling myself as a student at Georgetown, something I half jokingly admitted to considering. Her phone number, or even her last name, were not among the many tidbits of information gleaned that morning. We strategized that my best move was to hope for another "metro moment," as he called it, tongue in cheek.

At noon I complained of a headache and revealed in an emotional display to the congressman's chief of staff my genetic predisposition to migraines. Then I left early and hovered in front of the large bank of newspaper machines at the subway entrance, stalling for over three hours as I prayed to see her embark on her homeward commute. I alternated between pretending to talk on a payphone and crouching in front of the rusted blue boxes reading the display copy of the *Post*, *Roll Call*, and two weekly papers I'd never heard of.

"Sam?" She approached me as I scanned the local headlines for the fourth or fifth time. "Can I loan you thirty-five cents?" She laughed. "Those newspapers aren't free, you know."

"Holly!" I said, turning toward the sound of her voice. "Well, well, what a pleasant surprise." I stood too quickly, suffering a head rush of near historic measure and nearly lost my balance.

"Whoa, Sam. Easy now." She put her hand on my elbow. "You gonna make it?" Her mouth and eyes smiled in near symphonic unison.

"Sure, sure. I'm fine. I guess I got up too quickly there."

"You been here long?"

I pretended not to hear the question and grabbed my dad's ratty leather briefcase.

In spite of the embarrassment, I suspected I was oozing glee at my scheme's sudden success. "Headed home?"

"Good guess, Sam." There it was again, the smile. "It's five fifteen."

"Then your chariot awaits. I had them hold the five o'clock." We rode back down the giant escalator, boarded the train, and headed under the river into Virginia, speeding along the tracks in the dimly lit tunnels of the subway.

"So, Sam, where are you off to this evening?" She was sitting in front of me with her head turned around and her arm fixed tightly on the back of her seat.

"Actually, I'm tied up in early dinner plans. I'm going to the finest hot-dog establishment in the greater metropolitan area."

A short pause. "Hot dogs?" As her head tilted to the side, strands of her long butter-blonde hair fell from her shoulder.

"Yes, hot dogs. I've got a date. A first date, if you must know."

"A date? At five"—she glanced at her watch—"at 5:37 on a Thursday?"

"Yes, a date," I responded firmly. "I've met someone

recently and I'd like to share the magic of a hot dog at my favorite spot. What's so wrong with that?"

"Nothing, I suppose, but what if your date doesn't like hot dogs?" We knew the dance was on.

"Granted, not all ladies appreciate the subtle flavor of the frank, but I sense this one is special. She has a certain . . . flickerivity." My straight face cracked. "I am willing to bet this lovely lady digs a good dog now and again."

"Flickerivity?" She giggled and covered her mouth.

At that moment the other passengers around us disappeared into the glow of the fluorescent lights above.

We were alone.

"Yes, flickerivity," I said with playful authority. "Look it up."

"You are too much, my subway stranger."

With no warning at all, on an otherwise uneventful day, I had found a way to make my life exceptional. Holly Elizabeth Walker would make it so.

We bounced along the tracks chatting about work, friends, and the painful fact that love had treated us unkindly in recent months. We approached my stop, and as the train creaked and cawed I stood and asked very officially, "Ma'am, would you dine with me tonight?" She said I sounded like a cross between John Wayne and a British butler.

Six minutes later I was buying foot-longs at River Dogs, a

one-man hot dog trailer tucked in a lookout area just off the Potomac River that divides Virginia from Washington. It sat in the shadow of my apartment building and had taken much of my disposable income through my first three years of college.

We sat on a hard, rain-stained bench for over an hour, slowly working on our hot dogs and overpriced bottles of water. I savored every minute, watching as the evening air and dimming light changed the tones of her hair.

"My heavens, what a sunset!" Holly said, looking up, her wide eyes marveling at the rich colors of the evening sky.

"To be honest, I hadn't noticed. There is so much beauty down here . . ." My voice trailed and I waited for her eyes to return from the skies.

"Why, Sam, you are a salesman at heart, aren't you? Well, my friend, my free advice to you is to look up from time to time."

"Look up? Why look up? The world happens down here. Life happens on this bench, where we control the game, the moves. Sure, the skies, the clouds, they can be beautiful and all. But I'd hate to lose myself up there while I lost my footing down here."

Nice one, Romeo, I thought as I gave a swift kick to my dangerous ego. *Dumb, dumb, dumb.*

"Sam, Sam, Mr. Jaded Sam." She cocked her porcelain face to the side. "I see I have some work to do here."

We exchanged telephone numbers, e-mail addresses, and finally our own last names, a forgotten detail we laughed at. I escorted her back to the subway and off she went, headed home to campus and the research project that awaited.

That was just the first of many perfect dates. There were minor league baseball games, church activities, days on the beach with friends we now shared, and a weekend trip by bus to meet her mother and sister in Charleston. Most memorable were the countless late-night sessions about politics, family, miracles, and heaven.

The most important date took place six months later, sitting on the same bench and ending with me kneeling in front of her with a modest solitaire diamond ring. She stared into the black velvet box, tears stuck in her eyes. It seemed I waited an eternity for this moment—and for an answer.

Finally she put her fingers on my chin and carefully pulled up my head. "Look up," she said as she kissed me. "Yes."

✳   ✳   ✳

We were married on the one-year anniversary of our very first riverside date. We celebrated our honeymoon right in our own backyard, downtown Washington, D.C., staying in the nicest room we could afford at the Watergate Hotel. We had both lived in the area for years but never taken any significant time to see the city and enjoy its history. So for six days we slept late and saw the sights.

We toured the White House, the Washington Monument, and the Lincoln and Jefferson Memorials. We acted like tourists, asking directions to buildings we stood in front of, having real tourists take our picture dipping our feet in the U.S. Capitol's reflecting pool. We were only minutes from the Tyson's Corner apartment we now shared, but for all we knew we were thousands of miles from the busy lives that awaited us at honeymoon's end. Holly teased that if we made more money we could cancel our new lease and live in that famous hotel forever.

I often wish we had.

The early months of our marriage passed in a joyous blur and we settled into comfortable routines. Holly was finishing her dissertation, and I was debating whether to pursue a master's of business administration or get right to work. Financial realities, most importantly the mountain of student debt we shared, made the decision an easy one.

By our sixth month anniversary I had graduated and was proving myself at a computer-networking firm. I sold myself in the interviews as the future of their sales department. It didn't take long to deliver. I was paying the bills—and then some—before my ninety-day probation was over.

I could sell.

Meanwhile, Holly earned her doctorate and we celebrated back on the banks of the river. We sat cross-legged on a red-white-and-blue blanket her mother had made as she'd sat in a comfortable chair in the community room of her retirement home. We ate hot dogs and cheese fries, gloating in the perfection of our lives.

Two weeks later Holly accepted a full-time teaching position at the only university she'd ever known. I lobbied for her to take time off, enjoy her accomplishments, spend time with her mother, or visit her sister in New York. She refused. She was determined to contribute to the nest egg already established for anyone that might come along bearing our same last name.

It turned out that someone was coming sooner than expected. By our first anniversary Holly was already eight weeks pregnant.

In April of the next year Holly was overseeing a study group that had gathered to discuss an approaching exam on eighteenth-century British literature. "Mrs. Foster! Are you okay?" One of her students interrupted from a table in the front row.

"Sure, of course, why?" Holly answered with a grimace, clutching her podium with both hands.

"Because your skirt is leaking." Holly's water broke during a passionate speech on test preparation, priorities, and time management. She confessed later to feeling labor pains for hours but being concerned that her students were still unprepared for their first college final.

"So, class," Holly said, smiling with embarrassment at their most unusual predicament. "Are you ready for the exam?"

"Are you ready to let a dozen college freshmen deliver your baby?" the witty young man answered.

"Very well, then, would someone kindly call a cab?" They called an ambulance instead. Holly delivered our baby boy somewhere in traffic between campus and Saint Luke's Hospital.

"I'm so sorry you missed it," Holly said from her bed in the maternity ward.

"Nonsense. You gave those young minds an education money can't buy." I sat at her side, awkwardly cradling our crying, pink newborn.

"Honey, why don't you pick the name?" she said, squeezing my hand.

We named him James.

CHANGES

James Samuel Foster was born as perfect as one can be in this imperfect world. He had a full head of jet-black hair, beautiful dark brown eyes, and the requisite number of fingers and toes. He grew into a slender young man, not an ounce of fat on his wiry frame.

"Enjoy it while it lasts," Holly loved to say. "One day you'll wake up and every chocolate chip cookie will cost you another inch in your pant size."

From his first of many babysitters, a sweet retired couple that lived next door, James developed a love for all things that float: boats, fish, and anything small enough to fit in the toilet. When he was four we caught him saluting the Three Stooges—the family goldfishes—as they swam with the current and were swept away in the toilet of the guest bathroom. Holly told him the magic pipe would take them on a much-needed special vacation and that soon they would return refreshed. Two days later three identical goldfishes appeared in the fish bowl, now well out of his reach.

In his first week as a bright-eyed kindergartener, James found the telephone number of a new friend on a class list. He locked himself in the laundry room and called the student's mother to ask that she encourage her son to stop calling him Jimmy. "My mom and dad named me James for a reason," he said boldly. "And I would be happy if Stephen, who's really, really nice, by the way, would call me James."

That boy could make things happen.

By our tenth anniversary, James had unwittingly become the nearly exclusive source of happiness in our home. Our marriage, like most, we reasoned, had grown stale over the years. I spent as many as twenty days a month on the road, constantly trying to break sales records or crack the tough client everyone else feared. I was deeply in love with my job and the success that being on top had afforded us. I'd "set the bar high," I told Holly, cleverly evoking that excuse as easy justification for the long hours away. Even when the schedule landed me home, I was often unavailable, in constant planning for the next client conquest.

To her credit, Holly achieved similar successes in academia. Each semester she taught as many classes as the chair of the English department would allow. She published several articles a year and was courted constantly by other universities for prestigious fellowships. But she wanted to be the youngest professor ever awarded tenure at Georgetown and was well on her way. Holly loved teaching more than anything; she once told her sister that she was the mother of reverse polygamy. "I'm married to a new round of students every semester," she joked.

She defined devotion.

By the time James turned ten he was spending far more hours with our network of trusty sitters than he did in his own home. He had become a sensitive young man, sensitive to a spirit of goodness and kindness, unusually tenderhearted for a boy his age. He was not perfect, not by any means, but we recognized maturity beyond his years. Even the funny old ladies on our street loved him. "He's a real lady killer," they called out whenever we crossed paths outside. They spoke of arm wrestling one another for the right to sneak him off to Las Vegas when he was eighteen.

James loved the attention.

They loved him.

Foster family outings had become a rarity, not by design, but by fates of scheduling. The highlight of James' tenth year was his small, family-only birthday party. "I don't need a big party," James told us. "A family party would be best anyways."

On my way home from the office that evening I bought him a wood carving block and a long-promised first pocket-knife. While he and I sat on the front step learning to whittle a simple boat, Holly fashioned a sail out of a small piece of red material and white string. She returned to the porch, sail in hand.

"How's it coming, boys?" She smiled at the block of wood James was hacking on. "Hmm, not quite a boat yet, is it?" she offered playfully.

"No, Mom, but it will be! And it will sail!"

"My dear, I'd put money on it," Holly replied and leaned down to my ear. "Sam, if that thing sails," she whispered, "it will be a miracle." Before the night was through, the once-jagged block of wood resembled a genuine sailboat. Holly dubbed it *James' Miracle*, and painted the name proudly on its hull.

James set his alarm for five o'clock the next morning, grabbed his Popeye flashlight and book bag packed with a thermos of milk and two chocolate cupcakes, and walked carefully through the dawn fog toward a tiny creek that ran through the neighborhood.

"It sailed," he called, running in the back door and up the

stairs to our bedroom. "It sailed!" He flung open our door and launched himself in between us. "It really sailed!"

"Never a doubt in our minds, James." Holly wiped a dollop of cupcake cream from his cheek. "Never a doubt."

We were all three healthy, happy, and in our own worlds. Holly and I liked to imagine that friends watched us and saw the perfect family. We were successful and almost always smiling.

That is, until a random Thursday afternoon.

✳   ✳   ✳

I returned from a lunch meeting to find the president of our company and his vice president of sales in my office. There had been a board meeting, company revenues were down, the economy was sputtering, and costs were being cut to ensure profitability before we ran in the red. In five minutes I went from being the highest paid salesman in their history to the newest member of the unemployment community.

My success there had earned me a generous salary, but now they were choosing to gamble by promoting a much less expensive junior associate. It was no longer about loyalty; it was about costs. They offered a severance package that would provide a few months of stability while I searched for work. We also enjoyed some family savings that we always hoped would pay for college and retirement, not groceries. Nevertheless, having it there was a comfort.

They continued speaking in their well-trained corporate tones as I dumped knickknacks into a white cardboard box. "You should be proud, Sam. You've been an enormous success," said the CEO. "But it's come at a very high price to the company."

And to me, I thought, standing and shaking their hands in disbelief.

Twenty minutes later I finished a few good-byes and, with an escort, exited the side door toward the employee parking lot. *Keep your chin up,* I thought. I had been the escort before and seen more than my fair share of departure tears. *Chin up.*

✳   ✳   ✳

I took the long way home, in no way anxious to walk in the front door and report on my afternoon. Driving by my old apartment building by the river, I snickered at the ripped awning still hanging over the front door. I pulled into my parking spot and recalled long-dormant memories from the years when life's greatest worry was how to spend a Friday night. "A movie or dancing," I said aloud, staring up at what used to be my living room window. "What'll it be, Sam?" I closed my eyes and gave in to visions from what felt like a previous life. One at a time I pushed aside the movie reels of my mind, each one taking me further back and closer to Dad. It didn't take long before I was back in the eighth grade at a parent-teacher conference. The scene was as crisp as the night I lived it.

"Good evening!" Mrs. Erekson sang the words and shook Mom's and Dad's hands, then mine. "So good of all the Fosters to join us this evening. Sit, sit." Mom sat where the teacher gestured, but Dad bypassed the gray folding metal chairs for a small student desk next to mine. He pulled an array of painful faces, wedging himself tightly in, ignoring Mom's embarrassed giggles.

They exchanged small talk: The school cheerleaders were traveling to a regional championship in Philadelphia; one of the guidance counselors was retiring after thirty-eight years of service; the librarian was recovering nicely from a fall on the newly refinished floor of the teachers' lounge.

"That's all terrific," Dad interrupted. "So, how's my son?" He loved cutting to the chase. I shifted nervously, picking covertly at what felt like chewing gum cemented under my seat, and prepared for the worst.

"The news is good, Mr. Foster. Your son is the epitome of satisfaction. Everything he does in eighth-grade English is perfectly . . . satisfactory." Ouch.

"Certainly there is something—" said Mom, but Dad quickly interjected.

"No, dear, please, allow me." Dad winked and Mom suppressed a grin.

"Satisfactory?" He paused for effect. "Satisfactory? This boy is anything but satisfactory. He's extraordinary." Dad slapped me on the back and fumbled his way out of the desk, nearly tumbling over its top. "Thanks for your time," he said politely, regaining his balance and reaching for Mother's hand.

The conference was over.

* * *

A knock on the window pulled me back to the present. "Hey, move it, buddy. You're in my space." I pulled away and drove ever closer to home. *Just one more stop.*

One last short detour put me under the bright lights of the batting cages next to the complex Holly and I had lived in after that magical honeymoon a lifetime ago. I spent ten dollars in quarters beating oversized softballs to a pulp. "I will not be out for long." I swung the aluminum bat like Babe Ruth, punishing each pitch. "I will not let them beat me." I connected hard on another and smashed it high and deep into the mesh netting. "It's time to reopen *The Sam Show*."

* * *

Holly was pulling a box of ragged library books from the trunk of her car as I pulled in the driveway. "Hi, Sam, could you get the door?"

"Let me carry that." I reached for the sagging cardboard box.

"No, I've got it. Just the door, please, Sam."

Just what we need, more junk for your dust collection. I held open the door and listened as she struggled up the attic ladder to find a spot for another donated box of useless books.

Better tell her tomorrow, I thought, settling into the den to begin reconstructing my stale résumé and freshly battered ego.

ACCIDENTS

It was a day like every other in the three weeks since losing my job. I dropped James off at school and spent the morning hours sending e-mails and making calls to check the status of a few long-shot job opportunities. That afternoon I made a cold call in person to a technology-lobbying firm in Washington. As expected, they were not hiring, but if something changed I would be the first candidate they called. By now I had been told I would be the first one called for a hundred different positions.

Winding my way through heavy traffic and across the Roosevelt Bridge back into Virginia, I heard my cell phone ringing in my briefcase in the passenger's seat. I fumbled to open the case, steering for a moment with my knee. Finally the phone was at my ear. "Hello, Sam Foster."

After an uncomfortably long pause, "Sam?"

"Yes, this is Sam. . . . Hello?"

"Sam." It was Holly. Another few seconds of silence passed.

"Sam, I am at the hospital."

"Hospital? What? What hospital?"

"Sam," her voice cracked. "It's James," she gave up the effort at composure.

"Holly, calm down, please. What about James? Where are you? Where—what hospital? Are you in the emergency room?"

"Saint Luke's. I am at Saint Luke's." My wife, a woman I had only seen cry a few times in our entire marriage, was now sobbing. "I am in emergency, the emergency room, at Saint Luke's. Come, Sam. Please come."

I spoke each word slowly, "Holly, what . . . has . . . happened?" But in between her sobs there were no discernible words, only despair.

"I'll be there in fifteen minutes."

✶ ✶ ✶

Arriving at Saint Luke's, I found Holly sitting on an outside bench in front of the bright red emergency room entrance. She pulled her head from her hands and sat up as she heard me call her name. I sat beside her and she slowly unraveled the details of the evening.

She had returned home from the university and picked up James from the sitter, an older woman who was more of a grandmother to James than merely a babysitter. She was always his favorite. Before Holly and James arrived at our own front door Holly remembered a stack of essays she had meant to pick up on her way out that evening.

"Hey, captain, would you like to come to Mom's work for a minute?"

"Sure!" he'd answered. Time with his mother outside of the house was a cherished commodity. They returned to campus, quickly retrieved the essays, and drove through James' favorite hamburger spot for cheeseburgers and chocolate shakes.

"We were getting onto Lee-Jackson," she said without looking up. "James was already working on his shake. . . . A truck, a landscaping truck, came behind us off the ramp and lost control merging into traffic."

"Oh no," I whispered. "No."

"He tipped sideways, he landed on us, from the right, the right side. James was pinned and they couldn't pull him out." She was crying again, shaking visibly, holding tightly to her hair and bending toward the ground. "They wouldn't let me watch, Sam. They put me in an ambulance, and I sat there listening to the metal saws cut him free. Sam, I'm sorry. I'm sorry." She rocked back and forth.

"It's fine," I offered. "Everything is fine. I'm sure it wasn't your fault." I silently hoped that was true.

"He was driving too fast. Sam, I could tell he was. I knew it." She calmed a bit and I rested my arm on her back. She melted into my lap.

She had called 911 and almost instantly an ambulance, two police cars, and a fire engine had arrived at the scene. The landscaping truck was on its side, and rich green sod littered the highway. Stunned motorists slowed and stared at the mangled wreckage. A city bus driver that had seen it happen from behind stood as close as they would allow, arms folded, shifting his weight methodically from his left leg to his right and back again. His passengers huddled near windows, watching in silence from the idling bus pulled over on the ramp's shoulder.

The rescue squad, on the radio with doctors at Saint Luke's, determined en route that he would head straight into surgery. The trauma to his head and neck were the most severe of his injuries. Holly, miraculously, she felt, suffered only scrapes and bruises and a badly sprained wrist. We believed all her injuries would heal with time.

We sat for thirty minutes, awaiting news from inside. Memories of our ten years as a family of three raced through our minds, images flashing in our eyes like old filmstrips: Summer days in Amish country or at our favorite campground;

fall afternoons, barbecuing in our backyard; James bringing a blackbird he named Pirate in from the outside, most of his left wing missing from a battle with a feisty neighborhood cat. I saw myself in the car, just days ago, picking James up from a Saturday sleepover with a pal from school. They had raced their boats in a man-made fishpond in their front yard.

*   *   *

A voice startled us from behind. "Hello, excuse me, are you the Fosters?"

"We are, we are." I jumped up and spun around. "What can you tell us? Where is he now? Is he out yet?" I grabbed Holly's arm, much harder than I meant to, and pulled her up to her feet. Seconds later we were being seated in a small seafoam-green waiting room. The nurse shut the door behind us.

"Mr. and Mrs. Foster, your son is still in surgery. The doctor asked me to come down and give you an update. He thinks we will be in surgery for another couple of hours if all goes well. And he thinks your son should survive."

"Oh, thank goodness!" Holly exclaimed. I thought the same but stayed quiet.

"There is, however," she continued very deliberately, "a possibility that when your son emerges from the anesthesia he could require continued life support to breathe. We do not know quite yet, but there are some signs."

My heart nearly stopped.

"They would like you to be near the recovery room, so that if there is some time, even a few seconds as the anesthesia wears off, that you can see him while he is alert."

"Are you telling me that he may not know me again? Us?" My voice was uncharacteristically shaky. "Are you saying he could never wake up?"

"Sam, don't!" Holly's words bit the air. "That's not what she is saying . . . Nurse?"

"No, of course I am not saying that." She chose her words more carefully now. "I am here to tell you that the doctor . . . the doctor asked that I come down to tell you there is a risk, yes, a risk, that your son could require life support following the surgery. Given his condition and the severity of his injuries, it is possible."

We stared at her, hanging on every word for a reason to keep faith, something to justify a dose of hope.

"Mr. and Mrs. Foster, you know, we are lucky he's alive," she said.

"This is luck?" I said sharply, revealing a temper I had long ago learned to control.

"We are doing everything we can; you must know that.

Please believe that." She put her hand on Holly's arm. "I'll be back soon. I will ask the emergency room managing nurse to keep this room closed for you. It's not much, I know, but it's some privacy."

She opened the door, turning as she stepped through. "I will be back." And she was gone.

Holly rested her head on my lap and wept. I covered her with my jacket and wished these moments of tenderness had not been so rare. The awkwardness was every bit as painful to me as the trauma we were ill-prepared to suffer.

$$* \quad * \quad *$$

It felt like hours had elapsed and the nurse had not returned. A glance at the clock above our heads told the truth: only forty minutes had passed. Holly had cried herself to sleep.

I put my hand on the top of her head and gingerly ran my fingers through her hair as if for the first time. I had met with corporate presidents, played golf with a governor and two congressmen, but I had never been more nervous than at that moment.

"Honey," I said loudly, hoping she would startle and open her eyes. "He's gonna be fine." I needed the silence to end. I needed to hear more about the accident.

"Is he? Is he going to be all right, Sam?"

"I don't blame you," I aimed for reassurance, "if that's what you're thinking." I missed.

"No, Sam," she replied, sitting up and fussing with her blouse. "I wasn't thinking that at all. But thank you for suggesting it." We were both pros at sarcasm, but I knew she must have been struggling with the notion that she was to blame.

"I was driving the speed limit. I was watching the road. I was—"

"I know, shhh, I know." I tried to comfort but without the slightest confidence. "We'll be fine; James will be fine. We'll get through this, we will." I had no idea whether I believed it myself and knew she must have felt the same.

Another hour passed and Holly somehow fell asleep again. I sat back in the hospital chair with my head resting against the wall behind me. In my mind I planned my next trip with James to the lake, the hobby shop, and the bookstore.

If only he might live, I offered. *I would take six months off, maybe more. I would take him anywhere he wanted. Rent a boat, sail the Chesapeake Bay for a week . . .*

My mind jumped wildly from the future to the past, and amid the flurry of memories fighting for attention settled my most favorite. Just a year before, my oldest brother had planned a joint family reunion for my mother, my brothers and their families, and various in-laws, including Holly's sister and her second husband. We stayed in three spacious log cabins at Wintergreen Resort in the mountains of western Virginia. All three cabins sat within twenty-five yards of an unusually warm mountain lake.

On our first evening there, before we'd even finished unloading the cars and minivans, James began selling me on the benefits of rowing him far out into the middle of the lake in our canoe to see if his small armada of toy boats would float in deeper, rougher water.

"Water is all the same; it's as wet out there as it is by the shore."

"Please? Please, Dad? It might be the only time we could ever test 'em." James was already a salesman.

"If it's so important, why don't you grab a life jacket and swim out there yourself?"

"Dad—"

"Son," I put my arm around him, "some things are worth swimming for."

James studied me and made his move. "You know, Dad. This is a special opportunity for a father and his only son. We could test our boats someplace they've never been; it's a true adventure. Why stick here close to the shore when you've got this canoe you rented and all these life jackets and the weather is super—"

"Oh, my! You're gettin' good, James Foster. You'll be selling sand in the desert in no time."

We donned life jackets and rowed out nearly a quarter of a mile, I estimated, to the center of the lake. James tied string to over a dozen ships and boats of every size and shape. One by one he released them into the choppy water. And one by one they turned on their sides, taking on water, and were gently pulled to safety.

The last boat to launch, *James' Miracle*, lasted the longest before it too was eventually swept over. Its sail floated flat and filled with a pool of heavy, dark water. James yanked hard and the string snapped in two.

"Dad!" James screamed. "I lost it!"

I swung my head around. "Oh no, captain, I'm sorry. We'll make another soon."

I turned back to the front of the canoe, and as I reached for the oars to paddle home I heard a splash behind me that was too big to be one last toy battleship. James' life jacket was sitting on the seat.

He wasn't in it.

"James Foster!" I yelled, watching him swim away from the canoe. "You get back in this boat right now. Right now!" It was mostly for show. I knew he swam like a fish, but I'd need the flavor of indignation when telling the story to his mother.

By now the tiny boat was out of sight and James was tread-ing water, mumbling to himself about currents and the wind. I watched him, and in a way I cannot explain, I admired his bravery. He was thirty feet from the boat now, catching his breath, floating on his back in fifty or more feet of water.

"Come on, James, swim back to the boat. Your mother is going to kill us both."

Or at least me.

"It can't be far, Dad. We'll find it."

"Good grief, son, let's go. You'll make another boat; we'll call it *Miracle 2*." I looked down at the floor of the canoe to hide an uncontrollable smile. I knew that child was not getting back on board without the only boat we'd ever made together.

"Stay there, Scuba Man. I'll come to you." I rowed the canoe back toward the spot where we had lost sight of James' six-inch wooden treasure.

I scanned the water's surface and drifted in circles while James dunked his head below the surface of the water again and again. As I made my case for calling it a night and getting him from the rapidly cooling water, James spotted a glimmer, a reflection on the surface from the last ray of the sun as it settled below the horizon. He swam toward it, chanting, "I knew it, I knew it. I told you, Dad. I knew it!" He picked up the boat and held it high above his head.

"Unbelievable," I said, paddling in his direction.

I pulled him in from the water, and as he wrapped his lanky arms around me, his blue, quivering lips uttered, "Dad, some things are worth swimming for." His teeth were chattering but his eyes were as bright as his boundless optimism.

"Tell it to the fish," I said, laughing like a devil and pretending to throw him back overboard. "Rescuing it was the easy part. Now you've got to explain this all to your mom."

We sang all the way back to shore.

* * *

Suddenly the door opened, startling us both and bringing me back inside the concrete walls of Saint Luke's. "Let's head up," said the nurse. "They are bringing him out now. Let's get you in scrubs and masks right away."

Holly was awake, wiping sleep from her eyes. We grabbed our things and followed the nurse to the staff elevator around the corner.

"Nothing has changed, Mr. and Mrs. Foster," the nurse began as the scratched metal door closed and the elevator began slowly rising. "The doctor still believes this is a very dangerous time. He'll come soon, I promise, and give you a proper rundown of precisely where we are."

The elevator stopped and we were led into a glass-enclosed

lobby at the head of the large recovery room. The smell was thick with memories of every hospital and doctor's office I had ever visited. But this time there were no smiling faces from nurses or secretaries, there were no lollipops in wicker baskets on the counters. This place in no way reminded me of health and life.

Quite the opposite.

We were asked to dress in white gowns, hats, masks, and even strange cloth booties for our shoes. I could not help but consider a quip about me looking like the Stay Puft Marshmallow Man. Long ago it would have felt so natural for me, but not lately, and certainly not today.

We followed the nurse through the next door and into the buzzing room. Light green curtains separated the beds like a makeshift prison, and round white lights hung from the ceiling on thick steel rods.

"James!" Holly exhaled loudly as one of the curtains was pulled back, revealing what was left of our vibrant son. He was attached to more tubes and machines than I would allow myself to count.

"My boy," Holly said, falling to her knees and holding on to his arm rail.

"It will be some time still, but stay close." The nurse disappeared and again we were left alone, on each side of James' tremendous bed. He was a thin, helpless boy lying in the middle of a sea of sheets and tubes. It reminded me of the adventurous Tom Sawyer and his wonderful raft. I hoped James would have a chance to make the same observation for himself later. His spirit would light up at the irony.

As another hour passed, we alternated between holding his hand, sitting on the side of his bed, and staring at the bank of digital machines that seemed to be counting the remaining seconds of his life.

"Look at this," Holly said, running her fingers along the edges of the gauze strips that covered his head. At his sideburns the bandages were sheer enough to see his bare scalp. "They must have shaved him."

"Hair grows back," I answered, barely audible. Another long space was stolen by silence.

"He'll breathe again, Sam. I promise." She stroked his scraped forearm, one of the few pieces of skin not covered by bandages or electrodes.

"He's breathing now." I was always in charge of the obvious.

"You know what I mean. He's going to recover; he's going to live again." She was speaking louder than she realized.

"Shhh . . . but what if he doesn't? What if he never wakes up? What if these machines are all he ever knows?"

"Sam, Sam, Mr. Jaded Sam," she said slowly. "It's about time we had another miracle, don't you think?"

I felt a hunger to pray, to hold Holly's hands and plead for James' life, but time and distance had blurred the memories of our early-marriage bedside prayers. *We should pray*, I thought over and over, hoping she would somehow hear and offer the suggestion herself.

She didn't, and years of accumulated pride made me keep the idea to myself.

As promised, the lead doctor explained in detail the surgery and the trauma to James' head. The prognosis was not good, he explained. His survival rate was fifty-fifty but with only a slim chance that he would ever breathe on his own.

Suddenly our makeshift prison felt like death row.

BEGINNINGS

The sun rose through a window over Holly's head, but on this overcast day it was hard to tell. A new day had arrived, but James had not come back.

He was moved to a private room on the same floor. During the next few days, Holly and I left that room only once for more than a minute or two. Holly asked me to run home to get her some fresh clothes and stop by the university to pick up some books and assignments from her office. I was never lonelier than that day, driving down streets and highways, unaware of where I was, forgetting more than once why I was out at all. Every street sign reminded me of my broken life and every song on the radio spoke of second chances at life and love.

As I sped over the bridge into Washington I realized that

my drumming on the steering wheel, something I'd learned to do to distract myself from anxiety, had turned my palms and fingers red. *Perfect,* I mused. My hands were throbbing, rain was falling, and the radio was blaring my least favorite Beatles song.

Rubbing my temple with one hand and steering with the other, I remembered that my first-aid kit, a recent birthday gift from Holly, contained a small package of aspirin. I reached behind me into the backseat, but instead of the green plastic case, I felt the sail of *James' Miracle*. He had sailed it at his friend's sleepover.

Without thinking I pulled the boat from behind me, opened my window, and flung it toward the pavement. I watched in the rearview mirror as it crashed and cracked along the road, eventually slipping beneath the guardrail and falling far into the river below.

What have I done . . . ?

* * *

Back at the hospital we watched for a sign, a moment when the hum of the machines around the room would be silenced by the sound of James' voice calling for us. Each passing day chipped away at those hopes. Days turned into weeks.

Holly would soon have to take a formal leave of absence

from the university. It broke her heart, but she felt she belonged in James' room. "When he wakes up I will not have the first person he sees be a shift nurse who doesn't know his name." She would tell me that a thousand times.

I became engaged in near daily battle with the insurance company. Without the courtesy of informing us, my previous employer had apparently cancelled our health coverage before I'd even left the parking lot, and now they maintained that the window for self-coverage had closed. We would fight on, but the bills would not wait. Even with insurance, Holly and I were already living on savings and planned to cash in my retirement account. Soon we would need to liquidate our life insurance into cash as well. The last to go would be James' college fund. Dipping into that would be an admission neither Holly nor I was yet willing to make.

Holly and I were not spending much time together any-more. We had not eaten a meal together or had a meaning-ful conversation about anything other than James in nearly a month. The consequence was a marriage growing weaker by the day. At times it felt like we were dying alongside James, day by day, little bits at a time. The rare chats were in muted, emotion-less tones about the weather or money or bills or moving on.

What would we do if he never woke up? At what point could we both be away from the hospital at the same time?

When could she return to work without feeling guilty? Each day ended with more questions than answers.

* * *

The truth is, I'd first suspected Holly and I were falling out of love a few years ago when on our anniversary, instead of an evening out, Holly had essays to read and I had a business trip to San Jose. We determined to hold off until our schedules were more *in tune*. On a weekend not too far away we would celebrate our anniversary more appropriately.

We never did.

Through years of practice Holly and I had perfected an ability to peacefully coexist. We were two people living together but running our own, mostly independent lives, and sharing custody of the only reason we ever crossed paths: James.

In the three or four years before the accident there were few romantic adventures, movies, dinners for two, or midnight walks. There was only James. I began to find that, more and more, the reason I got in my car at the end of those fourteen-hour days was to see him.

I suspected Holly felt the same. On most days she would return home from the university, pick up James from whatever sitter was on duty, and retire to our bedroom to work at her small desk. She often graded papers or prepared for class until the middle of the night, then crawled into bed for a few hours before taking James to school and returning to campus.

Many of my evenings were spent in the den, researching prospective clients on the Internet or getting caught up on market and financial news. James would alternate between the floor in the den and our bed upstairs. He would read alongside his mother or sit beside me at his makeshift desk assembling a model or reading comic books.

We called him our "patient little captain."

✳ ✳ ✳

Without consulting much with Holly, I decided the time had come for me to seriously begin looking for work again. We were burning through our reserves quickly and I knew that regardless of James' health, I would have to work again soon. The medical debts were mounting, and though James' world might be coming to end, mine could not.

I needed something that would get me away from the hospital and from my own scars that I began to fear would never heal. Only work would help make me whole again. Happiness always came from being in the game.

A few days of searching the papers, the Internet, and the trade magazines turned up no obvious matches. I sent my newly freshened résumé everywhere. *Put as many hooks in the water as possible,* I told myself. *Someone out there is waiting for you to save them.*

The economy was in a nice recovery, or so they said, but my world was lagging behind. Every day the news was filled with stories of new hiring in the high-tech sector. The jobless rates were down, the stock market was finally sustaining a rally, yet every morning I awoke behind the curve. Sam Foster was unemployed and average once again.

Days came and went without me making extended visits to the hospital. I was weary of watching his skin become chapped and tough. Each afternoon Holly gently massaged his feet, applied moisturizer to his callused elbows, and combed through his now-permanently matted hair. Every day he resembled less my ten-year-old sailor.

He was becoming a person I no longer recognized.

After two weeks of disappointment and unreturned phone calls, I convinced myself that an entire day with Holly at the hospital would clear my head. We sat in James' private room, which was now filled by his many admirers with flowers, balloons, and candy he would never eat.

If it were me, I thought, examining the cards one by one, *I'd be lucky to get a cactus plant.*

Holly spent hours that day reading a book on Thomas Jefferson. I read every word on every page of the latest copy of

Forbes Magazine. Little was said, but, for the first time since the accident, I felt the slightest sense of peace, a subtle calm. It surprised me, but simply being in the same room together, absent the sobbing and stress, was a welcome respite.

Suddenly the silence was broken by a buzz coming from the front pocket of my pullover jacket slung over my chair.

"What is that?" Holly asked.

"It's my pager," I replied. "I left the cell phone home today; the nurses up front have been giving me a hard time about using it in here. Did it bother you? I'm sorry." We were both hypersensitive and anxious to avoid contention.

"No, no, Sam. I just didn't recognize the noise. I was afraid maybe we had a wild animal on our hands or something. You remember, James is allergic to pet dander." She cracked a smile at the rare joke, and for a flash I saw something familiar in her eyes: wit.

"I'll keep that in mind, Doc," I said with a half smile. "Let's see who's trying to track me down on a Sunday afternoon." I pulled the pager from the pocket of the jacket. The large text display read:

INTERVIEW
1753 ATLANTIC AVENUE
MONDAY 7:00 AM

I read it to myself again. "It says I have an interview."

"With?" Again her voice was refreshingly light.

"Oddly enough, it doesn't say. Just says 'interview' and gives the address." I read it again. "And it's at seven in the morning. That's rather unusual."

"I'll say," Holly added. "And who works at setting up interviews on a Sunday?"

"Must be one of the start-ups I sent my résumé to last week."

"Well, that's great, Sam. I'm glad."

"Yep, we'll take what we can get."

"Amen to that," she finished.

I slipped the pager back into its place and went back to my article in *Forbes*.

That night was spent home alone, again, and I had an especially difficult time falling asleep. The prospect of work was exciting.

And for a change I missed my wife.

Interviews

At five o'clock the alarm sounded with an old Bee Gees hit. I read the business section of the paper, quickly browsed the sports pages, and waited for Holly to call before heading out for the interview. I hoped she would remember and call with some encouraging words, but the phone never rang and I thought it best not to bother her. I grabbed my briefcase, my résumés and a thick stack of letters singing my praises tucked neatly inside, and made my way toward my first face-to-face interview since hitting the unemployment line.

I was grateful to have allowed extra time to find the obscure address. It was a very short side street in Arlington, just off the river, and more like a warehouse than an office building but with neatly manicured landscaping.

I pulled open the big door, stepped inside, and walked toward the receptionist's desk. There were three long hallways that met in the lobby. Like a spider's web they converged in the middle at exact angles around the room. I stood patiently, resting my arm and gently tapping my pager on the wooden counter atop the receptionist's desk. After three or four minutes I rang the small brass bell, and after another minute a man appeared, walking toward me from one of the long hallways.

"Sam Foster," he called.

"Sam I am!" I said, flashing my *Sam Show* smile. I had used this line to break the ice in sales meetings throughout the years. The man smiled back and nodded as if he'd heard it before.

"Come on back." I followed him down the same hallway toward a single elevator. We rode to the twelfth floor and exited into a large but mostly empty office. He motioned to an uncomfortable looking wooden chair right next to his desk.

"I'm sorry, I didn't get your name."

"Excuse me, Sam, I apologize. Call me Isaac. And welcome to GenTek."

"GenTek?" I repeated as we took our seats.

"Genesis Technologies," he said. "We are a consulting firm."

"Consulting—great industry. So what do you *consult* on?"

52

"That's a bit complicated, Sam. Very simply, we make other . . . enterprises better."

"I know that industry a bit. I know of a company in Richmond that takes consumer electronics from other companies and makes them more durable to abuse. Water, being dropped on the floor, kids, that sort of thing."

"Kids," he snickered. "There is no real protection against them, now is there?"

"No, sir, the peanut butter and jelly sandwich has done more financial damage to VCRs in this country than all other natural disasters combined."

"Right you are." He grinned. "Now if only we could weaponize that thing . . ." He laughed at his joke then leaned forward to become serious again. "Good, Sam. It looks like you are ahead of the pack, as always. Let's talk about you," he finished, and I settled into my seat, feeling at ease.

"As you know, I am Sam Foster. I have spent most of my life in the area. In fact, if you turn around you can see one of my old stomping grounds. I used to row on a crew team in high school. We spent many mornings—very early mornings—making our way up and down the river. We never won much of anything—that's tough to do when you spend as much time upside down in the water as actually rowing—but it sure was fun. Boy, we were one pitiful bunch."

"Regardless, what a beautiful way to start your day," he said.

"No question, sir, but in all those mornings, I must be honest, I never noticed this building here before."

"I'm not surprised. We only see the things we need to, right?" He swiveled in his chair and surveyed the view. The rising sun lit up downtown Washington. The morning line of light had arrived at the eastern shore of the river and within minutes it would burn off the fog that slowly rose from the cool morning water. "I admit I like coming into work early because of the sunrise. It's the biggest perk here."

"I bet it is." My knack for reading people served me well; we were off to an exceptional start.

"As I said." I took an aggressive move to pull his attention back. He'd become lost in the moment, gazing out his gigantic window. "I have been in the area for many years and I know my way around, both the streets and the business community. I have made a lot of connections and I sell well. I was laid off from a company not long ago—you know this crazy economy—and after a break I'm ready to get back in the game, your game, I hope."

"How have you spent your time off? Relaxing?"

"Actually, I've had some personal issues to deal with, so

I haven't done much of that." I wanted to avoid the topic of James. I needed no pity.

"Well, tell me about that last job, if you would, please."

"Yes, sir. I was working for a very successful, high-end software development firm. I enjoyed it, though I traveled a fair amount, sometimes twenty days a month."

"Wow, how did your family manage that?"

"They were . . . understanding."

"Were they? Lucky for you, then."

"I think they knew that certain sacrifices are required to compete these days."

Isaac smiled wryly. "You won't travel much here. You might take a trip from time to time, but we believe in keeping our team close to home. You're more efficient that way. You'll enjoy your job more. And you'll appreciate your boss much more." He emphasized *boss* and winked.

"I guess I shouldn't argue with that." I angled for a change in subject. "So, what do you expect I'll be doing? What are the duties of the position? Is it traditional sales? Would I have established clientele?"

"We'll get there, Sam. It's important we know more about you, what you stand for, and what kind of person you are. We might be called a peculiar group here. We are a tight-knit bunch. We fully expect—no, *demand*—our people become part of the GenTek family, so to speak."

"I can appreciate that. You don't find many corporations with that attitude these days. Sounds like an appealing place to work, at least from a corporate culture standpoint."

"Honestly, Sam, and this will sound corny, so brace yourself. We don't think of ourselves as much a corporation as we do a team. It works for us."

That was corny, I thought. But he seemed to believe it.

"Let me show you something. Follow me, would you?"

I trailed behind as we walked out of the office and down another long corridor. We exited onto a covered patio high above the river and overlooking the Capitol. "This is where I come to do my real thinking," Isaac said. "This is where I come when the days get rough. And I encourage my team, when days don't go as planned, to step out here and sit for a bit. It's a nice way to recharge."

I could only assume he was right. There were several people spread along the long, thin concrete deck. One man took notes on a yellow legal pad; another leaned against the railing, sharing an anecdote with a colleague; yet another sat at a small white table reading from a worn, leather-bound book.

"We don't have much of a break room inside so this is where we come to reenergize. There is something about this view and that river. But you know all about that, right?" I could tell that Isaac was the kind of man who believed every single word he said. *It's a rare quality*, I thought. I enjoyed it.

We stood staring out into the horizon. The Washington Monument stood higher than I remembered, and for some strange reason my thoughts were drawn to my honeymoon so many years before. Holly had bet me I couldn't make it to the top of the monument before her, and after some good-natured pushing and teasing, she did, in fact, beat me. But I remember it being worth it.

"What do you think?" His voice broke into my memories.

"I—it's . . . the view is outstanding." I struggled to organize my thoughts around what he'd been saying, not what I'd been remembering. "I must admit this all is very appealing."

"That's what we shoot for," he said. "Sam, can you show yourself out?"

His abruptness almost made me dizzy. "Um, yes, I suppose. Are we finished?"

"We are for today. I have another commitment and I've got to run. You're a well-qualified candidate, and I would like to think we will meet again, if you remain interested."

"I certainly am."

"Terrific! We'll be in touch." Isaac shook my hand firmly,

and before I could catch my breath, he was gone, moving through the door and disappearing from sight.

I found my way down to the front door. This time the receptionist was sitting dutifully at her station. She looked up from a stack of papers with a polite smile. "Thank you for coming, Sam," she said. I returned the smile and exited the quiet lobby.

✳   ✳   ✳

That night one of James' nurses persuaded Holly and me to escape for an "old-fashioned date," as she called it. "You two deserve it." She reminded us that I carried a pager and that a handful of fine restaurants were within a block or two of the hospital. Holly had become quite close to this particular nurse and it was clear they shared a special relationship. We decided that her quasi-marital advice hadn't crossed any lines and that maybe she was on to something.

Holly thanked her fifteen times, and we walked briskly to the Flaming Wok restaurant directly across the street. Chinese was not our favorite, but it was the closest.

We sat at the table nearest the front door beneath a cheap red dragon piñata. Holly positioned herself at an angle for a view of the hospital less than a hundred yards away. Seated in booths and at small tables around us were tired nurses and lab techs on break.

There's no escape, I thought.

Holly asked for the specials but then interrupted the waitress to ask which would come the fastest. She ordered for us both and we nervously twirled our chopsticks as we waited. It was the first time we had been outside our shared prison together. I weighed whether to mention that it felt like we were dating all over again, that the awkward energy was part of the courting game, but I knew she had other things on her mind. So did I.

"Tell me about your day," she finally mustered.

"Okay, well, I had that interview this morning, the one in Arlington."

"Oh, I'm sorry. I should have asked sooner. How did it go? This was the call you got yesterday, right?" She was surprisingly genuine.

"Yeah, it was . . . interesting. It's a place called Genesis Technologies. Out by the river near D.C. Very interesting company—quiet, very low stress."

"Would you be selling software again?" Holly asked.

"No, not really. They are a consulting firm, I think."

"You think? What exactly would you be doing?"

"To be honest, I don't really know yet. We spent most of

the time talking about me. It was unusual." The more details of the meeting I provided, the more I realized how unorthodox it had been.

"Well, it sounds very, very intriguing, Sam." Holly squinted her eyes and leaned her head forward. She spoke in the patented spy voice that used to thrill James and me. I'd not heard it or any of her other famous voices in quite some time.

"Intriguing indeed." I nodded back.

"So, you're interested?"

"I think so. We need to pay the bills, so whether I am interested or not, the time will come soon when we will not be able to afford being choosy."

"Sam, you know that if I could work, I would, right?"

I knew immediately where this could lead. "Yes, yes, I know," I answered quickly, hoping to avoid conflict.

"Do you? Do you know how badly I would love to teach again? Do you know how I miss the students? The faculty? Even the janitors, Sam. I miss it all. But I spend my days and nights in that room because James needs that."

We sat silently. "I am doing all I can," she added.

"Holly, I understand. He's mine too. I've spent just as much time worrying about him, about life without him."

"I suppose you probably have." She paused. "It is just that it's me who spends most of my life in that lousy room."

"If you are implying that I don't—"

"No, Sam," she cut me off, "I'm not implying anything. It's just hard."

It was not a fight, not really an argument, just another of many moments of tightly wound emotion. I wondered whether a real argument might actually do some good.

As if on cue, our food arrived and we ate in silence. Holly picked at her orange chicken and rice and we were reminded how broken our friendship had become. Even the simplest of conversations was now a challenge. What had kept our relationship intact over the last few years couldn't help now. He was wasting away across the street.

I cracked open my fortune cookie; it was empty. "Just my luck," I whispered.

We walked back without saying a word, both wishing we hadn't taken the generous nurse up on her offer. Holly would have preferred being at James' side, poring over medical charts, and I would have been content at home, scouring the web or newspapers for my next big break.

I said good-bye to Holly as we neared the automatic doors of the main entrance.

"You're not coming up?" Holly turned and asked.

"No, I need to get home. Need to keep looking, cannot put all my hopes on one interview. Need to generate more interviews, more chances, more opportunities." I avoided eye contact.

"What about us? You don't think we're an opportunity?" she fired back.

"Good night, Holly." I took a deep breath, turned my back to her, and walked away. Driving home I cried for the first time since the accident. I wondered that night if the Fosters would ever sleep under the same roof again.

ATTICS

The days passed with nothing more than a few meaningless interviews. Everyone was impressed but no one needed me. For the first time in my life I was down. The young, fearless intern who had wooed a beautiful college student all the way to the altar was gone.

I stopped visiting James regularly and when I did it was for a quick update from the doctors. Even then I often bypassed his room. James' home was now a sterile box with no sound but the steady hum of a respirator and the staccato beating of a heart monitor at his bedside. I doubted if he was even there anymore.

As the likelihood of James ever breathing on his own grew more and more slim, Holly revealed that the doctors had been discussing with her the possibility of "powering down" the life-support systems that surrounded his bed. They talked percentages and quoted studies. Holly politely listened but dismissed it all as hospital and insurance company economics.

It was a topic we had debated over the years whenever a famous case hit the news, but we had never given it any serious thought. We had been firm in our belief that "pulling the plug," as they always say, was not our choice. However, with my son now dying on the other end of those cords, I was much less committed.

I wanted his suffering to end. I wanted him to stand up. I wanted to enter his hospital room and see him sitting next to his mother, listening as she read his favorite book. I wanted him to eat with us, not from a tube but with the finest silver in the world. I wanted him to do more than just be alive; I wanted him to live! Yet each hour of each day proved to me that James was already gone.

He'd turned our lives upside down and left us to clean up the mess.

* * *

After two weeks of nothing from GenTek, I assumed the worst. *Get back to it*, I told myself.

I began scouring through old files in the den and ran across the name of a former colleague from Capitol Hill that I had interned with, Mr. All-American Kevin Farnsworth. Rumor had it that he'd made a fortune during the Internet boom and retired from the private-sector rat race to create a nonprofit think tank to address the challenges of small businesses.

I wasted no time tracking him down online and firing off an e-mail.

He responded within hours: *We have no budget for a star like you,* he wrote, *but let's do lunch. I'll crack open my address book and see what I can do.* I knew, if nothing else, he would be well connected.

Two days later I was standing in the lobby at his downtown D.C. office. "Sam Foster," he said, extending his large right hand. "How are ya, my friend?"

"Could not be better," I lied. "How are you?"

"Good, good. Come on in." He led me into his plush, comfortable office and pointed to an overstuffed leather couch. "Sit and tell me everything."

Kevin and I had spent only a semester working together a decade ago, but the connection was instantly fresh. We'd shared similar interests back then and caused more than our share of trouble together. We took turns recounting anecdotes for nearly an hour.

"You're well," I said. "I'm glad." I mustered as much sincerity as I could.

"Thank you, Sam. And it sounds like you've done yourself proud as well. I always wondered how you and Holly were doing. What's your son, ten, eleven years old now?"

I hesitated. "Eleven."

"Hard to believe, Sam. We're all grown up, aren't we?"

Kevin shared that he too had been married shortly after school but it didn't last. Within three years they had filed for divorce and moved on. "Maybe someday I'll try again."

I had thus far skillfully negotiated around the fact that my own family was dying in one way or another. I shifted gears. I was crafty at avoiding James.

"So, I need a job."

And with that, Kevin grabbed a notepad and began scribbling down names and numbers of former associates that might merit a phone call. We chatted briefly and then took the first natural break to wrap it up.

"They don't come more marketable than you, Sam Foster." He stood and slapped me on the back. "If things don't work out, you get back to me. I'll make calls if I need to."

He walked me out and we shook hands a final time. *So much for lunch*, I thought as I began the long walk back to the parking garage.

✳ ✳ ✳

Four blocks away and about halfway to the car I passed Dominic's, one of the older restaurants in town and one Holly and I had enjoyed many times together. *How long has it been, two years? Three? Why not? You've got nowhere to be.* I stepped inside and was seated immediately. I commented to the hostess that business was much slower than usual.

"They have no idea what they're missing out on, do they, sir?"

"You got it," I replied and began surveying the menu. A waitress came by and took my order for water and two lemon wedges. As she dashed away I felt a hand on my shoulder.

"Is that you, Sam?" I looked up.

It was Isaac.

"Isaac, how are you?"

"I'm great, thank you, Sam. Here alone?"

"In fact, I am. I just had an interview with a tech nonprofit and I thought I'd grab a bite before heading home." The fib was justified, I thought. Isaac had never called me back.

"May I join you for a moment?" Before I could answer, he was sitting. "An interview? Good for you, but I must tell you Sam, we've not lost interest."

"Really?" My voice rose.

"Yes, really," Isaac responded. "We've been wrapped up in

67

some important projects lately and have not taken the time to get back with you. I apologize for that."

"Certainly not a problem," I replied confidently. "I've kept my irons in the fire."

Isaac hinted that he too was there alone, and I invited him to order with me. We both had ravioli and a side of extra bread.

"I love this place," Isaac said, dipping a hearty piece of warm bread into a cup of marinara sauce topped with Parmesan.

"No doubt. It's been a favorite of ours for years. We used to know most of the servers' first names."

"You and Holly?" Isaac asked.

"Um, yeah." I blinked. I couldn't remember talking about Holly at our last meeting—at least not by name, but I must have. "My wife and I discovered this place while we were dating. Funny, actually, we were caught in a spring hailstorm and just slipped inside the door here to escape for a minute. Two dishes of lasagna later we were hooked. It's not the most convenient Italian place for us Virginia dwellers, but it's worth the drive now and again."

"Could not agree more," he answered. "They do it right here."

For a moment I couldn't speak, the memory of that afternoon was so strong. I swore I could smell wet pavement and the faint hint of Holly's favorite perfume. My stomach tightened, but I shook it off as just being sentimental. A lot of women wore that fragrance. We talked sports, grandparents, the unseasonably warm weather, and his desire to hit the nearest beach on the first day over seventy degrees.

"What a pleasure and surprise to run into you," Isaac said as he reached for the check.

"I'll get that," I said, pulling it across the table.

"How kind of you, Sam. But does this mean we have to hire you?" He smiled broadly.

"Nonsense, sir, but you do owe me a second interview."

"Fair enough," he said, and we left the now-bustling restaurant. "I'm off to a meeting on the south side of the National Mall. You?"

"I'm headed in that same general direction." I calculated I would walk twenty blocks farther than I had to, but a six-figure job would make it all worth it. We walked briskly and picked up on our lunch conversation; we shared stories about family and the opportunities we had both been afforded.

"Have you ever drafted an RFP?" Isaac asked, changing tack.

"A request for proposal?" Of course I knew.

"Yes, for new clients you've courted."

"I have," I said confidently. "But it's been awhile. Why?"

"I would appreciate seeing what you've done, to measure you against other candidates."

"Absolutely. I'll dig through the old boxes at home and send you a few. I think you'll be impressed."

"I'm sure I will. But just bring them next time we meet, if you don't mind."

"Will do."

"You've got a lot to offer, Sam," he said as we approached the reflecting pool at the steps of the Capitol. "I enjoyed this."

"Likewise," I replied.

"Let's talk again soon." Isaac continued on alone, walking with purpose down the gravel path toward the Washington Monument.

I sat for a moment on the granite bench at the edge of the shallow pool, watching my solo reflection flicker in the miniature waves. I cupped a handful of water in my right hand, let it slowly drain through my fingers, and tried to recall the last time I had been at that spot on my own.

I never had.

* * *

Late that night I stepped carefully up the thin pull-down ladder into the attic above the garage. "How long has it been?" I wondered aloud, moving from the top rung into the darkness, reaching out for the unseen chain switch to the utility light. I needed to find one of my old proposals for my next meeting with Isaac. Besides, the reminiscence our conversation had dredged up wouldn't seem to leave me be. I figured a quick trip down memory lane might be in order. And what better way to do that than in the place where nostalgias were kept.

The attic.

I gave the light chain a quick tug, and to my surprise the bulb still worked; a wave of unsettled dust floated across the beam of light. There were four sets of golf clubs, one of which had never been used; a still shrink-wrapped set of encyclopedias Holly bought for James on his first birthday; beach chairs; my record collection; a mountain of boxes including three marked CHRISTMAS FUN; and a sewing machine Holly took from her mother's when she checked her into the home some years ago.

In the farthest corner of the room I uncovered the only box I needed. Written in cherry red marker on its side were the words SAM'S STUFF. Even in oversized print across a slight tear in the box the handwriting was perfect. It was Holly's.

I opened up one of the dirty beach chairs, carefully sat, and began pulling off two layers of packing tape. Inside were manila folders marked TAXES (PRE-HOLLY), WARRANTY SLIPS, LEASE ORIGINALS, INTERNSHIP APPS, MBA BROCHURES, CC RECEIPTS, and BIZ MISC. I flipped through the last, looking for a specific proposal I'd written just months before moving into our new home. I knew it was well-organized, persuasive, and would do just the trick for Isaac and his team at GenTek. Mixed together in the inch-thick file were yellowed quota spreadsheets from my first job after graduation, folded commission slips, pay stubs, even a few stained lunch receipts from my first days as a salesman.

Then, tucked in between a ten-year-old quarterly sales report and the proposal I'd been hunting for, I found a sealed, white, standard-sized envelope that said simply, SAM, in that same cherry red marker.

Strange. Wonder what this is all about . . . I tore open the envelope from the side, pulling on the edge of the white linen stock paper and unfolding the trifolded single sheet of paper. I read aloud the first few lines but slowly quieted until the only noise around me was a faint buzz from a pipe somewhere in the dim space on the other side of the attic.

Dear Samuel,

It is almost midnight and the baby has finally fallen asleep. Perhaps I will enjoy a few hours of quiet before he wakes and calls for me again. By the count on the microwave clock James will turn one week old in twelve minutes. It's a miracle.

As I write this he is lying in his crib, snuggled in the

72

beautiful Noah's ark blanket my sister sent. You, my dear, are curled up in our warm bed down the hall, your legs pulled in toward your chest, your tired arms clutching that gross old pillow of yours.

Afraid I'll steal it in your sleep?

My two men, dreaming of big things to come.

Funny that even at this crazy hour, with my sore, baggy eyes, still wearing the maternity nightgown you'll tease me about in the morning, my men can make me smile.

Thank you, Sam. Thank you for sacrificing your back that afternoon waiting for me at the subway.

Thank you for sitting up with me night after night as I crammed to defend my dissertation. And for celebrating our success in a way I cannot ever forget.

Thank you for holding me tight and letting me cry on the day we found out James would be coming. (Much earlier than we planned!)

Sam Foster, when the sun shines tomorrow I will love you.

When the clouds come and the sun seems farther away than heaven, I will still love you.

When we are old and slow and sitting on a porch swing, I will tell you for the millionth time of my passionate distaste for hairy toes. And I will love you more than ever.

> *And you will always love me back.*
> *That is our miracle.*

Forever, Holly

I read it twice more before catching my breath, drying my eyes, and neatly folding the letter and hiding it away in my shirt pocket.

I slept well that night.

CONNECTIONS

Two more weeks passed with no word from GenTek and no change in James. Holly and I rarely spoke except to coordinate schedules or transportation. We ate only a few meals together and it was largely by coincidence.

I wanted more; I wanted to try dinner again away from Saint Luke's, or a movie, or even a walk around the block in the natural light, away from that festering room that brewed anger and resentment. I asked once, while stopping by on my way home one evening from yet another first interview, if she could use dinner out, a walk, a trip to the store.

"I'm fine," she told me. "He's had it rough. His heartbeat has been irregular today and I hate to leave. I'd like to wait with him."

"For what? What are you waiting for?"

"A miracle."

There were other occasions with different words but the same result. She refused to leave the hospital together for an extended period of time. Even on the shortest trips she asked that I sit in her place.

Then, one evening, much to my surprise, she called the house to ask if I could spend the better part of the next day at the hospital so she could run a few errands. Most importantly, she said, was a trip to the university to fill out paperwork requesting an extension of her leave of absence. Even with her tenured position she'd heard that the dean was considering replacing her. Holly would fight. She wanted the university to be there for her if James ever woke up and the family could return to our routine.

I agreed.

I supposed that James' room was as quiet a place as any to read the classifieds. As the morning hours ticked away I began reading aloud to myself to break the silence. Doing so reminded me how much Holly enjoyed reading to James. I doubted whether it made a difference, but knew it did something for her; I knew it brightened her smile. So I riffled through the paper and began reading him the comic strips. First I read the captions, then described each frame in vivid detail. There was no reaction, of course, but there was something reassuring. *As long as his heart is beating there is a chance he can absorb something . . .* Or so I tried to convince myself.

After his hourly checkup from the nurse, I returned to the classifieds and began circling the ads with the most promise. Then James' tray table began buzzing on the other side of his bed. It was my text pager, bouncing alongside my keys and wallet. "What do you think? Good news?" I said to James as I stretched across the bed, careful not to put any weight on his chest. I grabbed the pager with my fingertips.

INTERVIEW, GENTEK
TOMORROW—7 PM
STEVEN'S STEAKHOUSE IN BALTIMORE
BRING SPOUSE

"James, it's good news indeed," I said with a spark. But Baltimore was a good drive away, and during Friday's rush hour it would be twice as long. My enthusiasm waned further when I reread the message. "Bring spouse." It was certainly not unusual for a company to want to meet the spouse; in fact, it was a sign that an offer could be extended on the spot. But convincing Holly to leave the hospital to travel over an hour away would be a Herculean task.

"Sorry, but if dinner with your mother is what GenTek

wants," I said to James, "then dinner is what they'll get." I would do whatever was necessary to persuade her.

I had lunch that afternoon in the hospital cafeteria, away from the room for just a moment or two, hopeful that Holly would not return while I inhaled a four-dollar ham and swiss on rye. Working my way through the maze of the hospital's basement, I passed the flower shop. *You could be back, Sam Foster,* I thought to myself as I stepped inside and bought a dozen roses and a crystal vase.

Shortly after four that afternoon, Holly returned. "Hi, Sam," she said, stepping into the room. "Thanks again. I got so much accomplished. Did you know there's a sun outside?"

"I've heard that." I was relieved at her good mood. "You needed the break, no doubt."

"New flowers? Who are the flowers from?" Holly picked up the flowers and spun the vase, examining the arrangement.

"A friend." I smiled.

"A friend? Sam, who are they from?"

"Me. They're from me. I thought the room could use something new." The sad truth was that the flow of flowers from James' well-wishers had come to a stop.

She scanned the room and saw the comic section sitting on the floor next to my chair. "It looks like a day here may have done you some good too. Were they funny today?"

"I read a few to him. He didn't laugh much." It was a risky thing to say but she smiled. Relief.

"No, he prefers adventure novels," she finished. It was a simple exchange like so many we'd had over the years, but today it was unusually refreshing.

I took my chance. "I got a message while you were gone today."

"A message?"

"On my pager, a text message." I tried not to look nervous as I readied the pitch. "It was the guy at that place in Arlington. He wants a second interview, over dinner."

"That's great."

"He wants you there," I said abruptly. "He wants you to join us. I'm sure they want to wine and dine us. It's pretty typical."

"What restaurant, how close?"

"It's great food. I'm sure you'd love it."

"Sam? What restaurant?" Her voice grew irritated.

"Steven's Steakhouse. In Baltimore." I held my breath.

"Baltimore! Why Baltimore? There is a Steven's here. Why Baltimore?"

"Honey, I have no idea. It was just a message. I'm sure there's a reason, but I can't exactly make a counteroffer to where we eat." I paused. "Sorry, I know it's a lot to ask."

Holly looked at James and then back at me. "I don't like it, Sam. Not at all."

"I know, I know. I'm sorry." I was surprised at how sincere I sounded.

Holly stared into space and we stood in a thick, mounting silence. Her countenance deflated. "The university is serious about letting me go even though I have tenure. Sam, I think I'm done there."

"Unbelievable. I can't believe those people are treating you this way. You're one of their own, for goodness' sake."

"It's all right, Sam; they have their priorities too. They cannot have my career waiting forever while I live in this room." Her voiced trailed off. "And heaven knows they weren't driving that night." She regretted saying it and we allowed a moment to pass.

"We'll do it. Steven's it is." She looked me in the eye. "But I want you to have that phone and pager ready. Straight there, straight back, no stops. And you better pray nothing happens while we're gone."

The threat did not amuse me, but I swallowed it. She was coming, and that was a victory I hoped neither of us would regret.

I spent that night home alone, again. I lay on my back in

the king-sized bed I hadn't made in weeks; Holly curled up on the recliner the nurses had set up ages ago in James' room.

I woke up early, got the paper from the end of our driveway, and read the stock market report from the day before. I showered, ate breakfast, and began watching the daytime hours creep by. *Keep it simple today*, I told myself repeatedly.

At three o'clock I put on my nicest suit, put the proposal I'd recovered from the attic in a brand-new folder, and stopped to buy a classy red power necktie on my way to the hospital. Holly ran home to freshen up and put on her best dress. She was back within the hour, and by four thirty we were on the Washington Capital Beltway making our way around the congested loop toward Baltimore.

"Not good, Sam," Holly said, looking at the mass of cars fighting to merge into traffic as we crossed the bridge into Maryland.

"They are all headed to Steven's," I said. "I must not be the only candidate they are meeting tonight." Holly grinned and looked out the window.

I turned to her favorite station, jazz, and a half hour passed with nothing but the music filling the car. From the corner of my eye I could not help but notice her soft pastel-green dress. I'd bought it in Houston a year ago as an "I'm sorry" for missing her birthday. She'd worn it only once.

What a shame, I thought but did not say. *She's beautiful.*

It was the comfortable silence we enjoyed when dating, when being near each other was enough.

"Do you remember the crocodile sign game?" Holly finally said.

"Oh, yes, of course I remember the crocodile sign game. How could I forget? I was king of the crocodile sign game."

"Give me a break, Samuel!" She rarely called me Samuel. "You were not king. I was queen, and you know it. My, my, where do you get your information?"

"It's the truth, Mrs. Foster, and you know it."

"Really? Do you recall a single time that you beat me?"

"No," I replied. "Not a single time, but I can recall several hundred."

"Ha! It's obviously been too long since we last played."

"Are you challenging me?" I said in my best gladiator voice, and we shared the first pure smile of the night.

"Absolutely. Let's go. Should I remind you of the rules, Sam?"

"Ugh," I muttered painfully but in jest. "If you must."

"Number one," she began. "All players must be in the vehicle at all times with the windows rolled up."

"What?"

"Quiet. Number two. All players must count only in their

native language. That's English for us, Sam. All other counting will be ignored by the judges."

"All right. Let's go, let's go," I taunted.

"Number three, all players must make their guess on the number of crocodiles *before* the buzzer sounds."

"We don't have a buzzer." I turned to her. "You made that one up."

"I know, and it's a travesty; we've always needed one."

Then we played what James had dubbed the "Crocodile Sign Game." We guessed how many times we would say *crocodile* in unison, between selected road signs. The counting stopped when the next sign was perpendicular to the car. The person who guessed closest to the actual number of counted crocodiles won. We had played that game many times driving up and down the East Coast over the years.

After five or six rounds, Holly's voice trailed off and she finally stopped counting between a speed limit sign and a billboard for a nearby Maryland Welcome Center. "James loved that game," she said, eyes glazed and staring out the window.

"Yep, he sure did."

"What a nut he was. Remember the way he'd count when he didn't win for a few rounds? He would guess a number much higher than we did, and then he would count real fast: 'one-crocodile-two-crocodile-three-crocodile,'" she said in rapid-fire.

"Then he accused us of being 'slow counters.'" Her voice trailed off.

"I think if I look over my shoulder in the backseat I will see him sitting there, holding a drawing pad and pencil."

"I know." There was another long stretch of silence.

"He's still with us, isn't he, Sam?" She sounded as if she needed convincing. "The doctor thinks his heart is still strong. He *is* strong." She pushed herself to be resolute.

Several more miles passed in silence. The traffic had finally lightened and we were at last driving the speed limit.

"Holly, do you remember that crazy trip to Niagara Falls?"

"Sure," she said. "It was before our first anniversary. That was the trip we had to have your mom wire us money to pay for the room. And it was just about the time you gave in and sold that clunker-mobile."

"Hey, now, that was no clunker. I loved that car!"

"Oh, I know you did, Sammy." She stuck out her bottom lip.

"If I close my eyes and concentrate, I can feel myself back on that boat beneath the falls. Remember that? Remember looking up? That cleansing sensation? The feeling of the mist covering our faces? Geez, that was fun. It's been forever since I've thought of that." I turned to see her head back on her headrest. Her face was relaxed, her eyes closed.

Half a dozen miles passed in a comfortable reverence. "So, do you think they ever found my wallet?" We turned to each other and laughed like schoolyard best friends.

* * *

We walked in the front door of the restaurant twenty-two minutes late.

"I hope he's still here." I was upset but tried not to show it. We approached the host.

"Good evening. Welcome to Steven's. May I help you?"

"We have a reservation, probably in the name of Isaac—" It struck me that I could not remember his last name, or perhaps I'd never asked.

"No, sir, no reservations with that first name at all. I am sorry."

"Try us, then. Sam and Holly Foster."

"Yes, sir, one moment." He studied again the oversized calendar resting on the wooden music stand.

"Yes, here you are, but I see a party of two only. Would you like me to seat you for three just in case your guest arrives?"

"Yes, please. I'm sure it's just an oversight. We'll sit, thank you."

"Very good, sir. This way." And he motioned with great

authority toward the dining room. I stuck my arm out and Holly took it. I could not remember when that had happened before.

We were seated at a table set for three in the farthest corner of the restaurant.

"You don't think he—"

"No, Sam, no. No one invites us to drive all the way to Baltimore, waits twenty minutes, and then takes off. He came through the same traffic we did."

"Maybe," I said. "But maybe he was up here anyway. Maybe they have an office here and it was just more convenient. Maybe he got frustrated—"

"Sam, shhh." She made the sound and rested her finger gently across my lips. It was as pleasant a moment as we'd shared in months, maybe more.

And we waited. Fifteen minutes. No sign of my future employer. I was upset, angry that we may have wasted a trip a hundred miles from home. Holly told a story I'd never heard about a student from some recent semester who'd lost both her parents during finals week. I relaxed a little and revealed that I had bumped into Isaac at Dominic's just days ago.

Another twenty-five minutes passed. Begrudgingly I acknowledged that Isaac was not likely to arrive this late. We ordered a sampler plate appetizer with gourmet chicken wings and breaded cheese sticks. I told Holly that I had thrown James' favorite boat from the car on the night of the accident.

"He'll make another," she said.

Forty-five minutes more and we ordered our steaks. Holly told, in far greater detail than ever before, the details of that night. She chronicled every step they took from campus to dinner. "I was in a rush, Sam. I wanted to get James home in time for a cable special, a thing on sharks . . . I think I cared more than he did." Then she assured me, more than once, that she hadn't been speeding. She had taken off her seat belt to pay at the drive-through window and James had nagged at her to put it back on until less than a mile before the crash. In the seconds before being crushed by the landscaping truck, James told of a new student from Peru he'd befriended in his gym class. She recounted the last few minutes of their time together through warm tears; she rested her head in my hands atop the snow-white tablecloth.

After ninety minutes we shared a dessert called Decadent Chocolate Heaven. And decadent it was.

"Well, my friend," Holly said, sliding her finger across the plate and mopping up the last of the chocolate fudge. "It would seem that you—excuse me, *we*—have been stood up."

"I'm afraid you're right," I responded. "I'm not sure

whether to be disappointed or grateful. It's crazy, really, but this has actually been pretty fun, yeah?"

"Yeah," she answered. "But if you don't mind, I would like to get back."

"You don't think there is any chance that he still—"

"No, Sam." She shook her head. "There's no chance." We paid a ninety-dollar bill we couldn't afford and began the long trek home. Holly was asleep three miles onto the beltway and I realized it was the first time I'd seen her sleep since the accident.

I secretly wished for another traffic jam.

MYSTERIES

I brought Holly her favorite breakfast the next morning: fresh orange juice, an everything-bagel with low-fat cream cheese, and a single piece of dark chocolate.

"Good morning," I said, swinging open the door. Holly was seated in her usual spot, reading through a new medical journal. "I bring tidings of good joy . . . and food."

"What a nice surprise; thank you."

"Nonsense. I should be thanking you. You took a gamble last night driving up there with me and I wanted to thank you."

"Sam, that was no gamble. The real gamble was marrying you in the first place."

"Ouch," I shot back. "That'll hurt later." She stood from her chair and approached me.

"You're welcome." She hugged me in a way not familiar to me for months, maybe more.

"How was the night?" I asked, sitting on the side of his bed as she dropped back into her seat and began unwrapping her bagel.

"Uneventful, really. Still nothing new. The doctor did come by again this morning to drop off another brochure or two and ask if we'd talked further about long-term plans."

I knew what she meant. That was the hospital's way of asking whether we had given more thought to removing James from life support or moving him to a facility that specialized in terminal patients. They were bringing up the subject every week or so. The choice was still ours; but I knew in time it would be taken from our hands.

"And? What did you say?"

"The same thing I said the last time they asked. I told him we feel strongly that, one way or another, he will pull out of this." She looked down, speaking with a matter-of-fact, newsreader tone that signaled she was unwilling to debate.

It had been some time since we'd had this discussion and I was unsure whether we were prepared to have it now. I was reluctant to test the strength of what may have been a mild thaw between us, but with the doctors increasing the pressure to make a decision or move him elsewhere, I knew it could not be avoided much longer. I plunged my hands into my front pants pockets, a nervous habit from my grade-school days. My right hand felt a folded piece of paper and I pulled it halfway out. It was the letter from the attic. I curled it into my palm. "You really still feel that way?"

"I do, Sam. I do. I cannot picture sitting here one day as some nameless doctor or nurse flips a switch, or pulls a plug, or whatever it is."

"I understand. . . . At least I think I do."

"That's not a lot of confidence, Sam. I know you better than that."

"I am trying to understand; I really am. But do we still believe he might actually wake up one day? When can we sit together and say that it would be better to see his suffering end? I've been thinking, and hear me out now—why not reconsider and look at other options? Bringing him home? Taking him to a place that is better equipped for this kind of thing?"

"This kind of thing? What? People who were injured in car accidents?"

"Of course not—"

"Sam, you don't bring a sick person home to recover, not with these injuries. Hospitals are best equipped to deal with the changes in his condition."

"Changes? What changes?"

"Bringing this boy home or checking him into a death motel somewhere is giving in, Sam. We'd be giving up, saying there is no chance he'll ever breathe fresh air on his own."

"Come on, now, look at him, would you? Don't you want this suffering to end someday?" I knew full well the trap.

"He's not suffering. You know that. There is no pain; he doesn't even know we're here."

"Exactly. That's right, Holly. He doesn't know we're here. He's probably gone already."

"Please, can we not go down this—"

"It's too late now." I quickly cut her off and regrouped to take a new angle. I recognized that this was fast becoming the perfect opportunity to make the case I'd been making in my mind for weeks. "I just don't know if we can survive much longer, that's all. When this is over, when it's just us again, I want there to be something. I want *us* to be *us* again. I've wondered lately if things will ever be the same."

"This is not about us! This is about our child; this is about the boy we promised to raise together. This is about being here for him." She was yelling now. "I'm waiting for a miracle, Sam. Are you?"

"Look. Look here. I believe in what I see, right here." I pointed at James, my index finger just inches from his face. "I see a young man that doesn't look a thing like me anymore." I spoke faster and faster as I moved across the room.

"Stay calm. Easy, Sam."

"No! I won't. I won't anymore. I'm upset, I'm tired, I am sick! Sick of feeling like I'm a single man again." Despair dripped from my eyelashes onto my brightening red cheeks. "I am sick to death of seeing you in this room and the smells and the useless optimism that gets us nothing but hurt week after week.

"Look here—he doesn't have your smile anymore, he doesn't have my eyes, he doesn't have a silly sense of humor. He's got nothing but a million dollars of computers connected every which way keeping him here longer than he should be."

I was crying in a way I hadn't known since that soggy day in the back of a black limousine. I wanted to pull Holly from her chair and hold her and tell her it would be okay, and I wanted her to do the same for me. But we didn't.

"Sam," she said, staring at her son, "I'll worry about you and me when James is well, whatever that means. He'll go— or stay—on his time. Not ours." Silence. "You know, Sam, we didn't exactly plan for this." The recovering joy of last night had evaporated in just seconds of thoughtless anger.

"I know. *This* is what we planned for." I tossed the letter into her lap. "At least I did." I turned and walked out the door. *I've gotten good at dramatic exits*, I thought to myself.

I pulled from the parking garage and began driving fast through the city streets. My head was spinning as I drove to the highway. *What is wrong? What is wrong with my life? When will this end? Will I ever have my life back?* I drove faster, weaving through traffic and honking at the slower cars around me. I drove for nearly an hour, entirely unaware of where I was going—of where I wanted to go.

A thousand thoughts and memories swirled in my mind and through them all came a perfect color image of my father. He was in his prized red cardigan sweater holding a travel-size package of salted peanuts in one hand and the steering wheel in the other. He was pulled over to the side of a remote two-lane country highway as smoke billowed from the hood of the family car. Gradually the moment grew familiar; we were on a summer vacation day trip to a working dairy farm at least twenty-five years ago. Mother was cross-stitching a picture in the passenger's seat.

Dad adjusted the rearview mirror for a better look at his Foster Four. "Children, sometimes you just have to ask," he said in his way that convinced us he knew everything, "for miracles."

On that day, and on many like it, Dad taught us that many

of the most heartfelt prayers he ever offered came when he was driving alone in our old Hornet. To and from work, to and from church, and on the many trips to school when I was too afraid to ride the bus. "Usually it's just me and Him . . . Plus, the way I drive, He's paying a lot of attention to me anyway."

That humid July morning, twenty miles from nowhere, Dad offered his thanks for our latest challenge and, with a milk jug and his lucky roll of electrician's tape, got us rolling again. The rest of us couldn't believe it, but we were milking cows by lunchtime.

"But that is not who I am." My mind returned to find an unfamiliar road before me. "That's Dad, that's his thing, his way." I drove faster, paying little attention to signs, lights, or the cars in my path.

"Where are you now? Huh? Where are the miracles now?" The louder I yelled, the more empty the space felt around me. I pulled off the road, cutting off a motorcycle and bumping hard into a truck parked alongside the otherwise quiet street.

"Terrific." I beat on the steering wheel until my soul ran out of anger. Steam rose up into the sky from the radiator and I wiped my eyes, only to have them well up again.

"Father," I said quietly, looking at a woman on the side-walk pass by and stare into the car. I nodded and waved.

"Father," I began again with more confidence. The word

was common enough but today it sounded like a language I had never spoken nor heard.

"Father, why is this happening? Why are we being put through this?" The air was thinning, becoming easier to breathe.

"Father, when will this end?" Nothing.

"Father! Why? Why are you not answering? Why are we suffering?" There were so many questions I had wanted to ask for so long.

"Why can I not find work? Why am I not needed? Why all of this? Why everything at once? Where is our miracle? Father, this is more than I can bear!"

My tone grew heavier. "Will my boy play again? Will he talk, or read, or laugh, or play the stupid crocodile counting game ever again? Will he *live* again?"

Tears flowed down my face, one by one collecting along my cheekbones and at the corners of my mouth. The salty taste and smell of grief took me back to the first pew at my own father's funeral. In the reflection of the windshield I saw myself at seventeen, sitting in an itchy black wool suit, staring at my oldest brother delivering a eulogy for a man too young to die.

"Father, what is Thy will with James?"

At last a quiet peace filled the car and a street sign out the passenger's window came into view. Atlantic Avenue. I was just a block from GenTek.

"I'll take that." I unbuckled my seat belt and reached for my briefcase in the backseat. "One thing at a time." I stepped from the car and looked over at the damage to my front grill without breaking stride.

I pulled open the glass door of Genesis Technologies and walked toward the familiar receptionist. "Hello. I'm here to see Isaac, and I won't leave until I do."

"Sir, I'm sorry, you are here to see who?"

"Isaac, I-S-A-A-C, the boss. I'm here to see him. Call him out here, please."

"Sir, I am very sorry, but there is no Isaac here. What company are you looking for?"

"What company? What is this? What company? Genesis Technologies. GenTek. Isaac is the man in charge, no?" I felt my temper flaring and I fought for a deep breath.

"Sir, please, please." She stood and came around from her desk. "We are not that company. It was GenTek, you say?"

"Yes, yes, this is the building, this is the where I interviewed for a job. What is wrong with you?" I sounded like an angry parent.

"Sir, we manufacture and market kitchen appliances—bread makers, blenders, that sort of thing. We're just moving in this week. We signed a lease on this building almost a year ago but have not been ready until now to actually move our people in." She put her hand on my arm, "Sir, the building has been vacant. I assure you this cannot be the same building . . ."

"Excuse me," I turned and ran down the hallway toward the elevator.

"Sir, stop! Sir!" She ran and called out to me, but the door closed before she caught up. I rode to the twelfth floor and the elevator opened into an empty room with a plain gray concrete floor.

"This cannot be." I headed for the exit onto the patio I'd stood on with Isaac. I brushed past a construction worker and pushed open the heavy door. There were no tables, no relaxing employees, and no playful banter. Just a few pieces of litter and a rain-soaked newspaper stuck against the fence overlooking the river below.

I leaned my chest into the fence and stared down at my feet. "What is happening to me?" I wondered aloud.

After several minutes I slowly looked up to see the sun catch something odd in the water below.

I leaned over as far as I could and there, floating in the river twelve stories down, I saw something floating bravely in the exact middle of the river. It was familiar.

What is that?

I ran back into the building and bypassed the elevator, sprinting instead to a set of stairs at the far end of the hallway. I leapt down each flight, touching only enough stairs to keep me from breaking a leg. I sprung open the door on the first floor and found myself on the south side of the building.

I moved quickly to the water's edge, looking up and down the river to relocate what I'd seen from over a hundred feet above.

There it was, fifty yards out and moving quickly downstream. Without considering the temperature or my shoes or the heavy jeans and sweatshirt I was wearing, I dropped my briefcase and jumped into the fast-flowing current. The freezing water stung my face and my lungs struggled to breathe in even the smallest gasps of air. A shot of adrenaline fueled my fight toward the mysterious object.

What is happening to me? Is this it?

I continued pressing forward, pulling the water to my sides, ignoring the hair glued to my forehead, at times shielding my vision. *You're a good swimmer, Sam,* I tried to say aloud, but the words stuck in my mouth. *Swim on.* I would not stop or go back until I knew what led me to the middle of the freezing Potomac River.

The object came closer into view. "It is not possible," I stuttered. The muscles around my frozen lips were twitching and my teeth chattered like a jackhammer. The noise should have been deafening. It wasn't. I heard nothing.

I reached out and pulled the small object in with one hand while the other treaded water more quickly.

It was a small, obviously hand-carved wooden boat with a simple red sail. On its hull it proudly read, *James' Miracle*.

✳   ✳   ✳

I have relived those moments a thousand times, maybe more. Though hard as I try, I cannot remember swimming back to the bank or crawling out of the river that day. I cannot remember how the car started or what route I took back to Saint Luke's Hospital. And I have never understood why, but as I replay those scenes in my mind, the details become richer and more vivid the closer I come to James' room.

I pulled into the emergency drop-off loop and left the car running.

I ran up the steps to the fifth floor and burst through the heavy steel stairwell door.

As I sprinted down the hallway to James' room, the sounds of my soaked sneakers squeaked and chirped against the reflective surface of the white-and-blue-flecked floor.

I pushed open the door.

Holly, looking like an angel, was kneeling at James' bedside in that beautiful green dress.

His eyes were wide open.

* * *

James did not sit up in bed that afternoon and ask for a tall glass of cold whole milk and a chocolate cupcake as Holly and I had dreamed he would. In the distant background no celestial choir sang hymns of glory. But Holly and I took turns positioning our heads carefully in front of his so that we could stare into his eyes.

That was music enough.

James died just before seven that evening. He sailed away on that massive bed with Holly and me lying at his sides. There were no last words, no final smiles, just an extraordinary lesson on chance, change, and miracles.

"He's gone," Holly whispered.

Isaac

Holly and I ate foot-long hot dogs that night from a grimy stand near my old apartment building. River Dogs was long gone but the cozy spot was just the same, and Holly joked that the food was as bad as always.

"Not so," I said. "It's never tasted better."

We sat on the same side of a picnic table overlooking the river. Holly took her last bite of dinner and final swig of water, and without a word, stepped up onto the bench, standing tall in the cool night air.

"Will you join me?" Holly asked as she climbed a step farther onto the tabletop.

"What in the world—"

"Oh, come on." She grabbed my hand and pulled me up. We lay back, side by side, on the top of the worn, uneven table.

We stared at the sky and its enormous blanket of stars. We were totally unaware of the people or minutes passing by.

"Sam," Holly finally said, "isn't it amazing what you can see just by looking up?"

I nodded, not really sure what she meant.

"Who was Isaac?" Holly asked. "If GenTek wasn't a real company, then who was he, and why the interviews?"

I had asked myself those very same questions. Had GenTek been some guy's idea of a practical joke? Or had it been something else? I have since tried to find any information I could about the company, but there were no records of anything by that name. No one named Isaac had even been associated with that building.

So who had I met? What was his agenda?

Did it matter?

In the middle of one of the worst experiences a parent could endure, Holly and I found each other again. That was the miracle.

And that was enough.

✳ ✳ ✳

Eighteen months later Holly gave birth to an eight pound, twenty-two-inch baby boy. We brought him home to a nursery painted with brilliant fishes in greens, yellows, and reds. They swim in deep blue waves of every size. Scattered around the room—and our entire home—are sailboats.

Lots of sailboats.

Today every boat in a river or ship at sea reminds us of James. Each one represents a struggle—how the will to remain afloat must always live. Over the years we have learned that in his unique way, James gave his life for us.

To anyone who will listen, and there have been many, Holly looks them in the eye and says that for each true love in our lives, a small sailboat must be carved and painted. Each must sail strong on His water.

"It's not the size of the waves or the strength of the current. It's the power of the boat."

* * *

Our second son turns ten tomorrow. He will be given a block of unstained wood and James' old pocketknife. Together he and I will carve a sailboat, and his mother will make a simple red sail.

On the back in royal blue she will paint its name: *Isaac's Miracle.*